HEART'S REFUGE

Quinn Wilder

Harlequin Books

TORONTO • NEW YORK • LONDON
AMSTERDAM • PARIS • SYDNEY • HAMBURG
STOCKHOLM • ATHENS • TOKYO • MILAN
MADRID • WARSAW • BUDAPEST • AUCKLAND

Special thanks and acknowledgment to Quinn Wilder

ISBN 0-373-15298-1

HEART'S REFUGE

One

Casey Culver and the woman were alone in the cockpit of the Bell Jet Ranger helicopter he was flying over the remote wilderness of northwestern British Columbia. Her perfume wasn't assaulting him, like Delphine's always had. No, this scent came to him in small, delicate wafts, teased his senses, and made him uncomfortably aware of the woman he was so determined to be completely indifferent to.

His mood, already blacker than the thunderheads building in the distance, deepened to a shade of pitch. He wanted to ignore her completely, and he couldn't.

Caroline Pickford. He knew the name. He was even a little ashamed to admit he knew *Fame* magazine had picked her as one of the twenty most intriguing women in the world last year. He only knew that because his sister-in-law, Delphine—ex-sister-in-law—had been addicted to junk magazines, and now and then, if she left one at the office, well, what the heck.

The photos, mostly those blurry kind taken by some photographer hanging from a tree a quarter of a mile away, hadn't done her justice. Caroline Pickford was astonishingly beautiful.

He flicked her a look, resentful of her magnetism. Her spine was very straight as she sat beside him, her chin tilted at a haughty angle. She was dressed completely in black—silk, unless he missed his guess. The sea of black ended slightly below a shapely calf. Her hair was completely tucked up under some kind of black turban concoction that a lesser woman couldn't have worn. Her eyes were covered by oversize sunglasses. She exuded a potency that set his teeth on edge.

No wonder old Elroy Pickford, president of Pickford, Inc., arguably one of the wealthiest men in Canada, had ended his confirmed bachelorhood, at the age of sixty-seven, to marry her. It was disgusting. Even up here in the back of beyond they had felt the ripples of shock that marriage had caused. Delphine had chattered about nothing else for weeks. When had that been...five years ago? Six? The bride had been twenty-one. She didn't look twenty-six or twenty-seven now. Her skin was absolutely flawless, without even a hint of a wrinkle.

He shot her one more look, this time searching for signs of grief. No tear streaks. No ravaged look. No grief stricken gnawing on the sensual curve of pearly pink lips. There was but one slight sign of tension in that haughtily composed woman, he realized. She had a white-knuckle grip on the vaselike container she carried, and it was pressed tightly into her full swell of breasts so sensuous a few folds of gloomy black silk could not begin to hide it or contain it.

Elroy was in that vase.

Still enjoying the softness he'd bought and paid for, Casey Culver thought uncharitably. Not that she needed charity. She'd just become one of the richest women in the country. *Black widow.* He, of all people, knew enough to never let his guard down around a woman like this one.

She pointed and he nodded grimly. Just as she'd told his brother, Cord, she wanted to scatter what was left of old Elroy beside a northern lake. The one she'd pointed out looked like a puddle, but far be it from him to tell Her Highness there were more spectacular locations to be had.

No doubt she was only going through the motions of discharging her obligation to Elroy, before she settled down to the serious business of spending his money.

Starting with a nice fat fee to Culver Air, he thought with grim satisfaction. He realized he could fatten the fee a little more by suggesting a different lake, but he didn't need money badly enough to spend one more second than was absolutely necessary with this woman.

He put the helicopter down in a small clearing just beyond the lake. He looked out at the rugged wilderness of the far north of British Columbia. Another ten miles and they would have been in the Yukon. Some people would call this land bleak, with its endless array of swamps and stunted spruce balsam forests nestled between snow-capped mountains. Why would this landscape be chosen as Pickford's final resting place? From what he knew of Elroy Pickford, and it wasn't much, he'd been a corporate type—silk ties and Savile Row suits.

"Why here?" he asked, letting curiosity overcome the animosity he felt toward the very young widow beside him.

She didn't look at him when she spoke, as though he were some servant, intruding on her private world.

"He came hunting here once. He felt free here," she said softly, her voice husky and sensual, every bit as taunting as her perfume.

Men weren't safe with this one, he decided. He'd seen exactly what a bad woman could do to a good man. Cut his heart to ribbons, and leave him with nothing. His twin brother, Cord, had married Delphine, so blinded by her beauty that he hadn't been able to see how shallow and greedy she was. Like most twins, Casey and Cord shared a bond stronger than steel, and Casey felt Cord's pain over the breakdown of his marriage deeply, and with unforgiving bitterness toward Delphine. And he had a feeling this woman would make Delphine look like Little Bo Peep, given half a chance.

"Hurry up and do whatever you're going to do," he said curtly. "Storm's coming." He picked up a grubby old flying magazine, and opened the cover.

But he couldn't ignore how that dress slid up her leg, exposing the beautiful slender curve of her thigh as she got out of the helicopter.

He gave her a cold look. One Culver boy sacrificed on the altar of lust was quite enough. He resisted the temptation of making a cross of his two pointer fingers and holding them up like a shield in front of him. Deliberately, he brought the magazine level with his eyes, and noisily turned the page.

Caroline was aware that the man held her in complete contempt. It was not a reaction that was new to her, and she had learned long ago to harden herself to it.

'Who the hell cares what people think?' Elroy would say gruffly.

She did. But she knew how to make people think she didn't.

Deliberately she turned her back on the man sprawled out in the helicopter. She closed her eyes for a minute to clear her mind of his distinctly bristling presence. This moment belonged to Elroy.

She traced her fingers over the plain surface of the urn as she sighed and looked around. So, this was the country that he had loved. This was the place he had felt free.

She drew the crisp air into her lungs. Her eyes wandered over the landscape, untamed, rugged. Around the lake were stands of evergreens interspersed with thick brush.

"Just do it," that odious man snapped at her.

She turned and gave him a look, long practiced. The haughty look of a woman used to having her own way.

Though his wheat-coloured hair was short and neat, he was as rugged looking as the landscape. Where the hair touched his forehead it had been cut faintly crooked, as if he had grown impatient with it and chopped some off himself. His cheekbones were high and hard, his cheeks whisker-shadowed, the whiskers devilishly dark in comparison to the gold hair on his head. He looked to be thirty or so—he had a network of fine wrinkles starting around his eyes, hard eyes, blue as the waters of that lake, and just as cold. Those eyes were fringed by impossibly thick, dark, long lashes that emphasized the fact he was no doubt as sensual as he was strong and stubborn.

Sharing that confined space inside the helicopter with him, she had become aware he was not the kind of man it was simple to ignore. His was a potent brand of masculinity that made her heart thud too hard against her chest.

She'd been sheltered all her life, largely attending private girls' schools. She'd been so vulnerable to the strong feelings a good looking man could stir up in a healthy young woman.

Elroy had warned her never to trust that feeling of the bottom falling out of her stomach. He told her when she chose a man to choose him with her head, not her heart.

Not her hormones, was what he had actually said, crusty old curmudgeon.

She smiled slightly. He'd done his best for her. He had taken her in when she had no one else in the world. He'd protected her when she was young and silly and hopelessly romantic. Her parents had died in a plane crash her last year of school. Elroy, a close family friend, had moved in the same privileged circles as her parents, and had been made executor of the considerable fortune they had left her. She'd been left with too much money, and not enough experience to know how to handle it.

She'd thought she could mend a broken heart by outrunning it. She'd jetted here and there, and partied and bought outrageous cars. Then she met Bill Knight, a gorgeous young man, who thrilled her in every way. She lavished all her young love on him, and became engaged to him after a very short period of time.

"Hurry up!" the pilot snapped at her, then with a great rustling of pages, he disappeared behind his magazine again.

She turned again to the lake, and scanned it for the right place. She needed to be away from this bristling giant, alone with her thoughts, and her memories. Her gaze fell on an outcropping of rocks some way down the shore. She began walking.

"Hey, where the hell do you think you're going?" He'd come up behind her, so silently that his voice startled her. "Do you really think he knows the difference which patch of ground you pick?" His voice had a rough edge to it, an unpleasant sarcastic lift.

"Mr. Culver, you are being paid a ridiculous sum for this little excursion."

His eyes had narrowed to sapphire slits. "You are paying the going rate, *Mrs*. Pickford. Not everybody tacks on an extra thousand bucks onto their price when they hear your name. But my rates don't include guided hikes."

"Nobody asked you for a guided hike!" she reminded him with pique. "In fact, I'm quite prepared to pay you extra to leave me alone."

She was taken aback by the disdain in the blue eyes that raked her from head to toe.

"I'll leave you alone when we get to wherever it is you're hiking off to. Until then, I'll watch out for you." He looked pointedly at her feet. Flimsy black high heels daintily encased her toes. "Those are probably worth more than my entire wardrobe, but they're not exactly hiking boots."

He glanced at the sky. She followed his gaze. The thunderheads seemed frozen over the peaks of the distant mountains.

He gave her a disgusted look as he pushed ahead of her. He was wearing faded jeans that hung low on lean hips, and hugged tightly to muscular legs. When he turned around to make sure she was trailing like an obedient puppy, she noticed the left knee had been inexpertly patched. If this was an example, her shoes no doubt were worth more than his entire wardrobe.

The shoes were useless, and she slipped them off and walked quickly over the rough ground in her stockings, feeling that she had to keep the grueling pace he had set through the unforgiving bush.

"What is the rush?" she demanded breathlessly.

"Storm's comin'," he replied laconically, and picked up his pace.

Finally they arrived at the rock outcropping she'd sighted earlier.

He stood there, his arms folded over the great barrel of his chest, his eyes flinty.

"I'll leave you alone for a few minutes." The wind was picking up strength, and lifted his hair back from his head. He looked wild and free and strong. "A few minutes," he added curtly, and then walked partway back the way they had come.

She clambered up onto the rocks. The wind welcomed her as she closed her eyes, for a long silent moment, thinking of Elroy.

She'd been seventeen when he'd rescued her from the heart-wrenching intensity of her infatuation with Bill Knight. She thought Bill had loved her. In fact, he had loved the fortune she represented. Elroy had gotten rid of Bill with a well-designed lie: she had no fortune. And he'd bought her time to grow up with one more lie. He'd added a few years to her age, and made a public announcement.

The papers had had a heyday—broke heiress marries man forty-six years her senior.

By the time she'd felt ready to try it on her own again, Elroy had become comfortable with their arrangement. He loved her as the child he'd never had.

She gave up talking to him about leaving because it upset him, and he was in poor health. He was so proudly sure he'd found a way to protect her.

And in a way, he'd been right. She'd enrolled in university and finished school quietly. She became adept at ducking the papparazzi.

He'd protected her as best he knew how. She knew in many ways he was a manipulative and controlling man, but she'd come to love him anyway, with all his failings and his faults.

She opened her eyes and took the lid off the urn. It was exactly as he would have wanted it.

"Be free," she whispered. "Finally."

She tossed the ashes into the wind. He had made her promise she would not tell anyone about his deception until after his will was read. Tomorrow, she would be free, too.

Then she allowed herself to cry. She would miss him.

"We have to go."

Without warning her shoulders were caught in enormously powerful hands and she was spun around. Hastily, she wiped at the tears, tilting her chin defiantly at him.

He looked oddly...helpless, and almost of its own volition, a big thumb came up and scraped across her cheek.

His small gesture of kindness brought on a fresh wave of tears. The more she tried to control herself, the more it seemed her breath was coming in desperate gasps. Somewhere in her was a deep fury that Elroy, her protector and friend, had left her alone in this world.

The pilot pulled her into the hard wall of his chest. She went still against him, shocked by the steel hard strength of him, by her body's instant quiver of reaction.

"Did you really care about him?" he asked with soft disbelief.

She pulled abruptly away from the disturbing refuge of his embrace. She lifted her chin at the searching cynicism that had changed the hue of his blue eyes ever so subtly.

"My relationship with Elroy Pickford," she informed him with contemptuous softness, "is nobody's business but my own."

She did not owe explanations to anyone, and least of all not to this potently masculine man who stood looking at her with faintly derisive amusement twisting at his too sensual mouth. He was exactly the kind of man Elroy had been trying to protect her against.

The first raindrops splashed down around them. Culver turned abruptly on his heel, and began to walk, too fast, back through the dense growth.

Her feet hurt, she was getting soaked, her dress was now torn in more than one place and her hat was completely askew.

Culver stopped abruptly in front of her, and she crashed into him.

"What the hell?" he snapped.

She peered into the small clearing at the edge of the lake. She was relieved to see the helicopter.

Culver was running full bore toward the helicopter, yelling like an attacking warrior. A bear, silvertipped and absolutely enormous, tumbled out of the craft, reared up on his hind feet and sniffed the air. Culver screeched to a halt.

The bear made a sound that sent Caroline's heart rocketing into her throat. Abruptly Culver swiveled. He was coming back toward her, his strong legs pumping fast. His arms went around her, and he unceremoniously grabbed her waist and threw her against a tree trunk.

"Climb," he yelled, his hand immodestly placed on her backside, pushing.

To her own astonishment she went up that tree like a monkey, with Culver right behind her.

They found the safety of a tree limb, and Caroline inched out onto it. Culver came behind her, his hands steadying on her waist, as the bear heaved himself against the trunk of the tree. The whole tree shuddered.

She and Culver sat, breathing hard, and staring down at the bear, who stood up against the tree trunk and pushed on it with all his awesome strength until the tree began to rock and shake ominously. After a while he got down on all four legs and paced back and forth around the tree, hissing and grunting.

"What are we going to do?" she whispered.

"Wait him out." His arm moved around her shoulder, and gave it a hard, reassuring squeeze.

The bear made an ever-widening circle around the tree.

"I think he's leaving," she dared to hope out loud.

Holding her breath, she watched the bear trundle away, pausing occasionally to send an uncertain look back in their direction. He paused again at the helicopter, batted it a few times, and then moved on, his head swinging from side to side.

Her breathing slowly returned to normal. She realized how utterly ridiculous she must look sitting in a tree in a torn Paris original. She touched her hat. Somehow it was now on completely sideways. She laughed, pulling the hat from her head. Her hair, thick and dark, gleaming brown, tumbled down in a wild cascade around her face.

Culver's mouth dropped open. For a second, it looked like he was going to lift one of those big, callused hands and touch the astonishing abundance of her hair. Instead, he fixed those electric blue eyes on her face, and something hardened in his features.

"From the moment I laid eyes on you," he said harshly, "I knew you were bad luck."

Culver knew it was a rotten thing to say. But what else could he do? Even with streaks of makeup on her cheeks, the damned Pickford woman was so beautiful she made a man ache. Even a man as cynical and wary as he was. He watched the laughter die on her lips, watched them straighten out into cold, thin lines.

He reached toward her face. She leaned away from him, but their precarious seating on the branch wouldn't allow her to lean far enough. He plucked the glasses off the end of her nose.

His intake of breath was sharp and harsh. Her eyes were huge, fringed in an abundance of tangled black lashes. The irises were dark brown, glowing with startled innocence that reminded him of a wild fawn.

He understood perfectly why a man as brilliant, as cynical, as worldly as Elroy Pickford had thrown his legendary suspicion to the wind. After guarding his soul so vigilantly all those years he'd sold it eagerly to the devil. Because she had angel eyes.

He needed to get away from her, fast. That perfume again seemed to be swelling and filling the air around him. Casey Culver had gone up that tree fast, but he was off that branch and down it even faster.

"Aren't you going to help me?" she demanded.

Caroline Pickford was looking down at him with fierce pride. She turned around, and took a tentative step down onto the next branch.

"That's it," he coaxed, his voice a rasp in his own ears. He closed his eyes against the view. Unless he was mistaken there were very white panties under that very black dress.

She took another step backward. The skirt came down around his ears, silk brushed his face. His whiskers bumped into her soft, nylon-clad inner thigh.

"Get me out of this tree," she ordered tersely.

"Yes ma'am," he said, just as tersely. Out of this tree, into the helicopter, and out of his hair.

He reached up, ignoring her protest, and clenching his teeth, he wrapped one arm around her waist. Her waist was as narrow as the span of his two hands, and her breasts were full and pleasing as he pulled her down into his arms. He lowered her, none too gently, to the ground.

She didn't look at him. "This dress is ruined," she said, inspecting each little mark on the fabric with aggravating thoroughness.

As if she couldn't buy two hundred just like it tomorrow.

"You're young," he said. "It should be a long time before you attend another funeral...unless you marry another old man."

She stiffened, and looked straight at him. "Mr. Culver," she said icily, "I think I dislike you."

The words filled him with an unbelievable sense of relief. He swung away from her toward the helicopter.

They had been protected from the rain under the spreading branches of the tree, but now he noticed it was raining quite hard, the weather thickening all around them. He glanced at the canopy, and realized they were just going to have enough visibility to get out of here.

He went to get into the helicopter and stopped, frozen with one leg in and one still on the ground.

"Son of a sea-going serpent," he whispered.

Caroline moved past him. The silk of her dress was not holding up well in the rain, and was starting to feel mushy.

The interior of the helicopter had been trashed. Totally trashed. The control panels were smashed, the seats were shredded, debris and wreckage was everywhere. Aluminum was bent and Plexiglas shattered. The power of the bear was fearsomely evident.

She shuddered. "I'm glad he didn't get us," she murmured.

"Don't you get it?" he asked furiously, as if she was an idiot child.

"On second thought," she snapped, "I'm glad he didn't get *me*."

"We can't leave." She stared at him, at the way the rough planes of his face molded into lines of frustration.

He reached in for the radio, and came out with only the microphone, staring at the chewed-through cord with horrified fascination. Then he turned, took a step back, and with fierce strength hurtled the useless radio piece over the helicopter. It plopped into the lake.

She wanted to ask him what they were going to do, but the expression on his face made her bite her tongue rather than ask him. She was wet through to her skin now, and she began to shake.

"Here," he said. "Get in. There's no sense standing out there getting wet."

She obeyed him, because she sensed there was something more to the request than mere politeness.

"Will someone come looking for us?" she asked.

"Sure. Cord knew where I was going, within fifty miles or so," he said. "The ELT will bring them right to us."

"ELT?"

"Emergency locator transmitter. It gives a positive ID of our aircraft and also pinpoints exactly where we are. I'll turn it on manually." It seemed to her this miracle of modern science should have been causing a great more enthusiasm than it was. But she saw his gaze flick to the sky.

She looked, too, and understood immediately. She could no longer see the mountain peaks. The end of the lake was fast disappearing.

If she couldn't see out, a rescue team couldn't see in—or get in, either.

"How long do you think this will last?"

He shrugged his big shoulders. "Maybe a couple of hours."

"Why are you lying to me?"

He didn't deny it or have the decency to look ashamed. "Because I hate it when women panic."

She breathed in deeply, counted to ten, and pulled back her shoulders. "May I take that to mean, Mr. Culver, we have something to panic about?"

He looked at her, his eyes scanning her face. "The situation is serious," he offered slowly. "The long-range weather forecast was not good this morning."

"Meaning?"

"Meaning sometimes it socks in like this up here for a week—or two."

He said that last in a very low voice, as if he was rather hoping she would miss it.

"Oh," she said levelly, though her belly had just done a funny little skitter.

"I carry a survival kit."

He began to shovel through some of the mess. In a few minutes he handed her a sealed container about eighteen inches long and ten inches high.

It contained a small axe, fishing line, fire starters, a piece of plastic, a knife, a cooking container, tea, coffee and soup cubes.

"There's no food in here."

Culver picked something out of the survival kit. "This is food."

She took the bars from him and inspected them doubtfully.

"Ten thousand calories for every passenger," he informed her. "They taste like maple sugar." He then squinted at his lunch box, and pulled out a mangled sandwich. "Hey. He missed something edible. Incredible."

"Incredible," she murmured. Unless she was mistaken, the bear had taken a rather large bite before discarding it. "I'm not eating any of this," she informed him.

"More for me," he said carelessly. "We don't have very much food and you refuse to eat part of what we do have. This land is not kind to idiots."

She turned her face away from the contempt that burned in his eyes before he went back to his rummaging.

His mound of loot grew in depressingly small leaps. "We have a survival blanket, and some waterproof matches." He put what looked to be a tiny square of tinfoil on her lap, and a metal cylinder.

She watched him silently. His face was a study in grim determination. Finally he sank back into his own seat, and stared thoughtfully at the lowering sky.

"We've got some decisions to make," he finally said. "The supplies will get us through if we're only here for a couple of days."

She let the seriousness of those words sink in, though she didn't give him the satisfaction of seeing the deep fear his measured statement had caused in her.

"So what do you suggest?" she asked.

"We could wait it out, stay here."

But she knew he was not a waiting man even before he said his next words.

"Roads are few and far between in this country, but there's one about twenty miles from here."

Why did she get the uneasy feeling what he wasn't saying was as important as what he was?

"So, we can walk out?"

He shook his head. "Probably *we* can't. But if I left the supplies with you, I could walk out. I could probably be back before the weather even clears."

"Like hell." She didn't say that word often. It felt strangely satisfying. "You're not leaving me here. If you're walking out, so am I."

He snorted. "Yeah. Right. Power shopping in Paris is not exactly fitness training for a walk through the wilderness. And those silly things on your feet hardly qualify as shoes. You'll just slow me up."

"I'm not being left here by myself!" She closed her eyes and shivered.

"Caroline?" His hand touched her icy brow. It felt warm and dry and gentle. She shivered again, this time at the alarming way her body roused itself at his touch.

"Look, I'm not going anywhere today. We're going to have to get you warmed up."

She nodded gratefully. She heard a package rip. The space blanket settled around her and was tucked in. It felt like a plastic shopping bag, looked like a piece of foil, and crinkled alarmingly every time she moved.

"You're going to have to take the dress off."

Her eyes flew open. "I won't."

He stared hard at her. Finally he gave a shrug and a snarl, grabbed the survival kit, twisted in his seat, and went out the door.

So much for male dominance, she thought with bleary satisfaction. Take her dress off, indeed. No, they were much too close to their savage roots up here.

"Forget the ELT," he snarled a moment later. He appeared, holding a small piece of antenna, not even as thick as a coat hanger. "The bear snapped it off. It's useless."

"That figures," she murmured, the words costing too much effort. He gave her an assessing look, shook his head, and walked away with purpose.

It seemed he was gone a long time. She peered around for him, but could see him nowhere. The rain had painted the world a depressing shade of gray. She felt faintly panicky. Had he tricked her? Had he made her feel comfortable only to abandon her?

Just as that thought was taking hold, he broke from the trees and came across the clearing toward her. She felt ridiculously relieved to see him. He looked big and in control.

"Come on." He scooped her up into his arms. Instead of fighting him, she snuggled deep into his warmth.

He strode into the woods. A short distance from the helicopter he had found a small rock ledge, with a hollow underneath it. He had built a fire very close to it, under the shelter of the spreading branches of a large tree.

She went and stood by the fire, holding her hands out to it, feeling dazed and slightly drunken.

"Look, you're still soaked. You're still shaking. You're going to have to take off the dress." He was suddenly right in front of her, prying her numb fingers from the space blanket. "You take it off, or I will," he said. His face was impassive. His tone was steel.

Her head snapped back and she eyed him with all the defiance she could muster. It was pathetically little. She was cold. "Don't you dare," she said, with what strength she had left.

"Mrs. Pickford, I am not seducing you. I am not in the mood, even if you were the type to catch my fancy, which you most definitely are not—"

Instead of being relieved by that revelation, she felt oddly wounded.

"—and you have the beginning stages of hypothermia. You need to get dry and warm, fast. Am I making myself clear?"

When it was clear he intended to humiliate her by waiting for a response, she nodded, just barely. "Don't look," she said, fumbling with the buttons.

He sighed with exasperation, and turned abruptly. "Underwear, too," he said.

She was silent.

"I'm not playing games with you. If it's wet it comes off."

She fumbled with the clasp of her bra, and the wet lace of her panties. Finally they fell to the ground, and she grabbed the blanket and huddled miserably under it.

He turned. "In here." He guided her, none too gently, into the tiny shelter beneath the rock ledge. Somewhere he had found dry boughs and spread them out on the ground. She sank down on them. The fire was reflecting against the rocks and it was warm and dry in here. The blanket seemed to be radiating a comforting heat all of its own, though the shaking of her body would not seem to stop.

A moment later he was sitting, cross-legged, in front of her. Patiently he scooped soup out of a burnt black container for her. She didn't know if food had ever tasted so wonderful, so life-giving. The shivering began to subside.

She lay down inside the blanket, her eyes closed and she knew no more.

TWO

Caroline surfaced from sleep slowly. She became aware that the tip of her nose was cold. That the world smelled of pine boughs...and something else. A good smell, faintly tangy, like a spice-scented ocean breeze. The air was damp and cold, and she dipped her head under the thin foil blanket, and snuggled into the warmth behind her.

Her eyes shot open, and she felt her whole body go rigid. That smell, that good smell, was the smell of a man. And that warmth, that solid, comforting warmth was coming from him. From his *skin*.

Slowly, with disbelief, she rolled over. Her breasts brushed the matted hair of a very large chest. For a moment, she froze, the sensations coursing through her wild as a wolf's song. And just as compelling. And just as dangerous.

She came to her senses, and yanked the blanket off him, and tucked it around herself.

He started awake, and jumped up like he'd been burned, rammed his head against the roof of their rock shelter, and then staggered out into the morning, muttering and hopping as rocks dug into his bare feet.

She was thankful to see he was wearing underwear. She pulled the blanket into a tighter cocoon around herself, and glared at him with indignation.

"You were in bed with me!"

Understanding and outrage blended to make the blue of those eyes quite spectacular. "The nearest bed is about a hundred miles from here, lady, and you couldn't get me into it with you with a shotgun."

She should look away from him, she realized. But she didn't. He was a beautifully made man, all hard muscle and lean strength. A little shiver went up and down her spine as she thought about that big body pressed so intimately into hers.

"How dare you," she said with prim pique.

He moved toward the fire, and took his jeans off a line he had strung up. She watched with mingled relief and regret as he pulled them on.

She eyed him warily as he came back across that small clearing on panther feet. He ducked down and filled the space under the outcropping. His eyes were snapping blue sparks. He looked rough and dangerous, his light hair tousled, his whiskers nearly black in contrast. He looked like a perfect pirate.

"I was a perfect gentleman last night," he hissed at her.

"You wouldn't know what that is," she informed him.

"Is that right?" he said softly, his eyes narrowing to ominous slits. His hand moved, with lightning swiftness, and came to rest on the very edge of the blanket. He snapped his wrist and the blanket pulled away from her. His eyes did a lazy inventory of her breasts.

Her nipples hardened. She hoped he would think it was the chill air that caused that reaction, though she had the feeling it had more to do with the smolder of his gaze. A funny little firecracker went off in her lower abdomen.

He sat back on his haunches while she scrambled to cover herself.

"You bastard."

"You condemned me of a crime I hadn't committed. I wasn't about to wear the brand without having had the pleasure."

"We're not sleeping together again," she told him, trying valiantly to recapture some of her dignity.

He gave an eloquent shrug, then left the shelter. He took her dress and her underwear down from the clothesline he'd constructed.

"Get dressed," he ordered, tossing the clothing at her. "We have some miles to put on."

"I thought you were going to leave me here while you went for help." Her worst fear had become her most fervent hope.

A moment later he set that blackened container of soup in front of her. He broke off a chunk of the survival bar and tossed it down. "Eat." Then he strode away.

He should leave her, he told himself darkly. He knew he wasn't going to, though. She wasn't a survivor. She was like a rare hothouse flower and she was too fragile to make it up here if anything did happen to him on his way out.

He told himself that not leaving her had nothing to do with the sweet softness of her as she had pressed into him in the night, nothing to do with the lush fullness of her firm young breasts.

He sighed, and went back into the helicopter to see if he could salvage something else for the walk out. He grabbed the first aid kit, flares, maps and a compass. He stared with disbelief at something he had completely overlooked yesterday.

Peeking out from under the wreckage of the back bench seat was a black plastic bag. His laundry. He opened the bag and pawed through it. There were three sweatshirts and two pairs of jeans. Clean socks. And in the bottom of the bag, an absolute treasure. An old pair of canvas sneakers that he'd run through the washing machine.

Caroline was sitting cross-legged in front of the fire, trying to untangle her hair with her fingertips when he came back. He dumped the large plastic garbage bag in front of her.

Indifferently she opened the bag and peeked in. And then she reached in, buried her hands in the deep fleece of a large sweatshirt. She pulled it out and hugged it to her, then set it aside and went through the rest of the bag. Jeans, socks, sneakers! More sweatshirts.

She almost laughed out loud with delight. And then her delight died. She picked up the stack of clothes, and rammed them back into the bag.

"Where were these?" she said tightly.

"In the helicopter. I forgot totally about it. I'd taken a load of laundry into Dease Lake and—"

"You're despicable. You had all these clothes, and you made me strip and sleep next to you in nothing." And now she would never be able to get the imprint off her brain of how it had felt to have his flesh touching hers.

"I didn't remember the clothes."

"I don't believe you." She glared accusingly at him.

He took a step toward her. "My, what a high moral standard for a woman who put herself on the auction block and went off with the highest bidder."

Caroline felt the blood drain from her face. His words were strong, designed to wound. She grabbed the bag, and scurried for the privacy of the trees, her cheeks burning with fury.

She stripped off the dress hurriedly, and yanked a large navy blue sweatshirt over her head. It was wonderfully warm. She put on a pair of his jeans, and rolled them up at the cuff. They were huge through the waist, and she emerged from the bushes gripping them tightly with one hand, and holding her crumpled dress with the other.

He surveyed her critically, then took the bottom hem of her dress in between powerful hands, and ripped.

"What are you doing?"

He handed her a long strip of black fabric. "Do up your pants before they fall off."

She grabbed the fabric from him, threaded it through the belt loops and tied up the pants. With her hands clenched into prim fists, she sat on a rock, and haughtily inspected the tree line over his shoulder.

He came and knelt before her. "Is this more what you're accustomed to?" he asked. "Men kneeling at your feet?"

"Don't be ridiculous."

His glittering, mocking eyes held hers for a moment, and then he pulled her shoe from her foot. His big, calloused hand caressed her foot.

"What are you doing?" she asked through clenched teeth.

He shook his head with exasperation. "I don't know whether to pad the shoes, or put you in three pairs of socks."

Just quit touching my feet, she thought wildly.

Eventually, he used a combination of socks and padding, and the too-large shoes felt snug and warm. He then cut the plastic bag that had held his laundry, and made them both meager ponchos with it. Afterward he took her dress again, and put their scanty supplies into the full skirt, knotting it securely. He tied the arms around his neck.

"Let's move out."

The bugs were thick and horrible despite the thick, drizzly mist. The ground was uneven and roots tripped at her too-large feet. They had to climb over fallen logs and duck under branches.

A tree branch tangled in her hair and held fast. She gave a shriek of surprise, and reached back to try and untangle it.

She was bent over, struggling to get free of the branch, and seeming to get more hopelessly enmeshed, when he came around behind her. She could feel his fingers in her hair, surprisingly gentle.

"I'm going to have to cut it."

He took off the dress/pack, and found a pair of scissors in the first aid kit. He cut the tangle free from the tree, and she straightened painfully.

He stared at her, and then reached out and touched her hair. He raked strong fingers through the tangles. Having him touch her hair was almost as bad as having him touch her feet. He took one more long look at her hair and stepped back. He took the scissors and cut another long ribbon of fabric from her bedraggled black dress.

"Turn around," he said gruffly.

She presented him her back, and cringed against the quiver of delight that went through her when those large hands, with such uneasy gentleness, pulled back her hair, and tied it in the ribbon.

"Better?" he asked from behind her.

She could feel his breath on her neck, his fingers lingering lightly just above her collarbone.

"No," she said waspishly. "It would have been more sensible to cut it all off." She did not like the completeness of his power over her.

He caught her eye and smiled ruthlessly. "Let's move," he said, brushing by her.

"Yessir," she muttered under her breath. "Yes, master, sir."

They stopped at lunchtime. He handed her half of the ham-and-cheese sandwich she had vowed never to eat. The look in his eyes warned her not to even bother arguing. She was oddly grateful that her pride didn't have to do war with her hunger.

The coffee was strong, and sweet. They shared the container. Once or twice her lips even touched where his had touched and she seemed to be in no hurry to wipe them.

I'm losing my mind, she thought wearily.

They walked on. A long time before they arrived at it, they could hear the rushing of water. Then they were standing on a rough bank looking at a swollen creek.

"Damn," Culver muttered.

"What are we going to do?"

He looked at her and one corner of his mouth pulled upward. "Take off your clothes."

"You have a way of parting people from their clothes with unnerving frequency." She hoped that sounded smooth and sophisticated. She sniffed, and did her best to look away while he quickly shed his clothing and stood unself-conscious in all his male majesty at the edge of the water.

He hefted their supplies over his head and sloshed determinedly forward. The water hit his waist, and he struggled against the current, finally depositing their goods on the far side, and turned back.

He would probably never believe it, and probably nobody else in the world would either, but the truth was that Caroline Pickford had never seen a naked man.

"Your turn. Hurry up."

She held her clothes defensively in front of her until the water's edge. She closed her eyes and stepped in.

"Give me your clothes."

His arm wrapped around her naked waist and she clung to his strength as he held them both against the ravages of the raging water. It seemed to take forever, before, gasping, they emerged on the other side.

He shoved her things at her, and made a dash for his own as she shoved numbed limbs through uncooperative openings in clothes.

He got another sweatshirt and began to rub her vigorously through her clothes. Her skin tingled wherever he touched. He rubbed her colorless feet until she nearly wept with pain.

"You do me now," he ordered, handing her the extra sweatshirt.

His feet were blue. She rubbed them frantically with the shirt and her hands, coaxing the warmth back into them. Finally, she was rewarded when a faint pink began to creep back into the whitened flesh.

She glanced up at him. The dislike that burned in his eyes was so hot that she dropped his foot.

"Did you do that for your husband?" he asked, cold contempt lacing every word.

"What Elroy and I did together is none of your business," she told him icily.

A fire burned deep down in his eyes, turning them to sapphire sparks. But it was doused quickly.

"That's for damn sure," he said curtly. He could not explain the blackness that filled him.

Three

"Eat."

Caroline looked wearily at Culver. Eat? She was too tired to eat. Too tired to even be hungry despite the amount of energy she had expended today following that broad back through this endless wilderness.

"Mrs. Pickford—"

She hated the way he said that, with that bristling edge of sarcasm, as if the title Mrs. should only pertain to someone respectable, and she did not quite measure up.

Or maybe, she realized, slowly, she just hated being called Mrs. Pickford. She *wasn't* Mrs. Pickford. How she wanted that particular lie to come to an end.

She picked up the container of soup he had put in front of her. She had to close her eyes against the pleasure the heated broth caused her tongue. Her every sense clamored for more.

She opened her eyes. He was still standing there, big as a mountain. She had never been quite so acutely aware of a man as she was of Culver. His presence tingled across her nerve endings like the static before a tropical storm.

She was a little shocked at herself. Her parents certainly had not raised a girl who would allow feelings quite so...savage in herself. Even in that time after their deaths her wildness had gone to fast cars and parties. She had never been loose.

And much as Bill had appealed to her, his kisses had not made her think of heated skin touching heated skin. Though Elroy had recognized the danger of a young woman coming of age.

"I told them I married you," he'd informed her with satisfaction when she'd confronted him with the horrible rumors she had been hearing.

"But why?" she'd gasped.

"It'll give your head a chance to grow into your hormones," he'd answered in that blunt way of his.

She'd thought it was awful. She'd planned to tell everyone the truth. She wanted to rebel against Elroy's demand that she accept the protection of his roof, but she needed a place to feel safe while licking her wounds over Bill's callousness, feeling embarrassed and ashamed of how easily she had been taken in by a handsome face and a smooth line.

Later, when Elroy told her how sick he really was, she'd come to care for him a great deal. She couldn't

repay his awkward efforts at kindness by making him
appear an old fool in front of the whole world.

She finished the soup and the chunk of survival
bar Culver had doled out to her. He was stoking the
fire and his eyes met hers.

"Time for bed, darlin'," he drawled. "We have a
lot of distance to put on tomorrow." His eyes on her
were not the eyes of a man with resting on his mind.

With a haughty glare at him, she got up from the
fire, and marched to the lean-to. He had made a nest
of branches and the remainder of the clothes. She
slid onto them, put her head down, and closed her
eyes, pretending to sleep.

After a time he came into the lean-to. She could
feel her breath stop in her throat. *If he touches me,
I'll scream.*

The branches sagged underneath her. The strange
tinfoil blanket whispered around them. She sensed a
faint movement, and braced herself.

The tension was excruciating. The silence was tor-
turous. The minutes ticked by with horrid slowness,
and then suddenly she was aware the tension belonged to her alone.

The caveman's breathing had turned deep and
even.

For some reason she wanted to ball her hand into
a fist and smack him with all her might.

He woke up to find her curled up against him, his
arms looped protectively around her. Caught some-

where in between being asleep and being awake he was aware of a feeling of warmth deep in the pit of his stomach.

A feeling like a man who had been wandering through hostile lands, battered, tired, thirsty, hungry... alone. So very alone.

A man who had found refuge.

He cursed under his breath and yanked his arms away from her.

Refuge. He wondered if that was how Cord had felt about Delphine, poor sucker. No, there was no refuge in romance, just illusions.

Not that he hadn't had a romance or two. He was thirty years old. But he'd started his business when he was in his early twenties, and focused on it with a single-mindedness of purpose that had excluded all else. Women took energy. Lots of it. And families took time. He'd always thought, rather absently, that someday he'd want to settle down.

And then he'd seen what "settling down" did for Cord, and any ideas he'd had in that direction he'd quickly snuffed.

He stared at Caroline Pickford. Red warning lights were going off inside his head.

The forest was soggy with rain that day, and there was no sign of it letting up. Culver was setting a killing pace today. Caroline didn't have much food in her and as the day wore on her energy began to dwindle. He was pulling far ahead of her now, and try as she might, she could not catch up. He did not seem to care. She was too proud to ask him to slow down, and finally he was out of her sight.

She felt defiant and defeated as she sank down on the wet forest floor. Her feet hurt. She wondered when he would come back and look for her.

After a while a sound caught her ear. It came again. A shout? He was calling her name.

She got to her feet, and made her way in the direction of his voice. She was suddenly acutely aware that her survival was linked to him.

The trees came to a sudden end, and she looked out on a sea of swaying grass. "Culver?" she called as she stepped out onto the field.

She had not gone far when the earth turned spongy beneath her feet. She stepped to her right, trying to find dry ground. She screamed as she suddenly found herself waist deep in water and mud and sinking fast. The more she struggled the more the mud sucked at her.

He appeared suddenly at the edge of the grass, and she had never felt so relieved to see anyone in her whole life.

"Help me!" she screamed.

"Caroline," he said, his voice void of anger. "Calm down. It's a bog."

"Like quicksand?" she gasped, thrashing around.

"Caroline, stop!"

His tone did stop her, even though her heart urged her on. She seemed to remember a scene from a particularly ghastly movie where a man had met his demise when quicksand had sucked up his whole body and then folded slowly over the top of his head.

"Most of these bogs aren't very deep. Are your feet on solid ground?"

She focused her mind on her feet. Indeed, the sludge that encased them did seem solid. "I think I am," she said, never taking her eyes from his face. Of all the people in her life, he was the only one she would want to be with in this predicament, she realized suddenly.

"I need to find a really long limb to reach you with."

"All right." She said it bravely. "Hurry!"

He was back in the blink of an eye. Cautiously he made his way toward her. It seemed to take forever.

"Culver, what's your first name?"

"Are you joking?"

"No."

"What a time for introductions. Mrs. Elroy Pickford meet Casey Culver."

Finally he stood as close to her as he dared. Grunting with exertion he held out the long branch to her. After several tries, she grabbed it, and pulled with all her might. But it was his strength that released her from her muddy prison.

He pulled her across the remaining ground between them and she found herself in the fierce embrace of arms that still bulged with the strain of the effort he had had to make.

Then, without warning, his hands spanned her waist and she found herself tossed over his shoulder. He inched his way slowly out of the bog, and didn't set her down until they were back in the fringe of trees that surrounded it.

"Casey," she said tentatively, "thank you." She was aware of liking his name. It was slightly unconventional, which suited him. It was a strong sounding name.

She reached out and touched his hand. The moment their hands touched froze in time. She felt the warmth in his hand. The strength. The courage. She wanted to throw herself against him.

"Why didn't you ask me to slow down if I was moving too fast for you?" he demanded.

"I'm sorry. You have every right to be mad at me."

"I'm not mad at you, damn it!"

"Yes, you are!"

His face was suddenly very close to hers, his eyes flashing stormy sparks. "Don't you tell me how I'm feeling." He turned abruptly and took a step away from her.

"Get out of those clothes."

"But I barely know you," she said flippantly.

"That's right," he growled. "And let's keep it that way."

While he built the fire, Caroline peeled off her clothes. They were cold and clammy. Underneath her skin was streaked with mud. She stood before him, naked, aware in some primitive way that she was trying to punish him for his indifference to her.

He glanced at her. "You'll have to get cleaned up before you put on clean clothes. There's a stream right over there."

"I can't get wet again," she told him through chattering teeth. "I...just...can't."

With a sigh of long suffering, he strode over to her, tucked the space blanket tight at her waist, picked her up and tossed her over his shoulder. She felt too exhausted to fight him.

He carried her effortlessly, not missing a stride to pick up their one container. He ripped the blanket from her, and plopped her onto her fanny into the creek in one smooth motion.

The icy water hit her and she leapt up and tried to dash by him. "Let me go," she shrieked.

His hands were rubbing her wet skin, then sluicing the dirt off. The water was like ice, his hands like heated silk. It was the most sensuous experience of her admittedly inexperienced life. She gasped with shock when he rubbed rapid, cleansing circles on her inner thigh.

If he was aware that her trembling had changed in texture and was no longer caused solely by cold, he did not show it. His face was a mask as he leaned over and cupped cold water in his hands, tossed it on her belly and her breasts, until the mud was washed away.

And then the mask fell from his eyes and they trailed liquid fire as he looked at her with a primitive kind of possession, his eyes moving from her wide eyes, to the slender column of her throat, then resting on the full swell of her breasts.

But when he straightened the fire had been doused in his eyes. "You're freezing," he said. "We'd better get you warmed up."

He waded from the water, and picked up the blanket, and opened it to her. She came out of the water and he plunked it down on her shoulders, and then, moving fast, made his way in front of her, back to where the fire glowed.

The steady erosion of his control at the creek ate at his mind. She was damned near irresistible, soft and ripe, and utterly beautiful to look at. It could almost make a man forget she had ridden to glory on her face and figure, lured other men into her web. He had to get them out of this wilderness. This wilderness all around him, but in him, too. A place of savage needs.

She came out from behind a bush, clothed in dry things, and he ignored her, busied himself collecting wood for the fire, putting water on to heat.

She loaded some wood she had collected onto the fire, and dropped some soup crystals into the heating water. He liked it a lot better when she sat around looking miserable and acting helpless.

"The fire's big enough," he snapped, when she continued to collect wood and put it on the fire.

She sat down across from him, reaching for her portion of the soup.

"Do you have any family, besides your brother?"

He couldn't believe she was going to ignore his bad temper and make small talk. "Just my brother."

"I'll bet he's worried sick," she said sympathetically.

He glared at her. "Cord won't be worried. We're twins. He'll know I'm okay," he said uncomfortably. "He'll be able to feel it."

He thought of Cord's rocky courtship with Delphine, the misery of his short marriage. He had *felt* every single thing that Cord had gone through, felt it as though it was happening to him.

"He's special to you, isn't he?"

Damn her. Probing his soul with those soft eyes, seeing the vulnerable places in him.

"Yeah. He's special to me." He should have left it right there. He didn't. "He's just getting out of a messy divorce." He felt angry just thinking about Delphine playing his brother like he was a fish hooked on her line. "He married himself a gold digger who broke his heart, ruined him financially and walked away with half *his* company. He owns the fixed wing aircraft operation I share my hangar and phone number with."

"I'm sorry, Culver."

"Sorry?" he said with a snort. Sympathy had softened her eyes to velvet brown. "For who? Unlike you, she only got half."

He watched as the blood drained from her face. A direct hit, he saw, and wished he had the decency to feel bad about it. But he didn't. Her voice had been too soft and encouraging.

"How about you?" he said, pretending he hadn't been offensive at all. "Anyone worrying about you?"

"No," she said coldly, getting up. "No one's worried about me."

He watched her go, mesmerized by the sway of her hips and the hair cascading down her back in a rich black waterfall. Damn her. She'd gotten to him after all.

Caroline was not sure what had gotten into Culver. How could they go from the smoldering sensuality they had shared in the creek to this...armed camp, with such quickness?

Finally, tired from her ordeal that day, and exhausted from his growling and glowering, she retired. He followed her.

She was surprised when his voice came to her over the small space between them.

"Isn't there *anybody* worried about you?"

"Of course there are people worried about me," she said, too swiftly. And it was not exactly a fib. Mrs. Beckett, Elroy's housekeeper, had been very fond of her. But Caroline's experience with Bill had made it so difficult to trust the people of her own age group who were outside the circle of wealth and privilege. Elroy's assorted relatives—nieces and nephews—hated her passionately, perceiving her as a threat to an inheritance she suspected some of them had been busy borrowing against for years, so certain were they of their right to it.

"So, who's worried about you?" he probed.

She was silent.

"Family? Sisters? Brothers?"

"I'm an only child."

"What about your friends?"

"I told you. They're worried. Okay?"

"Sure. Name me some names."

"All right! Mrs. Beckett."

"Mrs. Beckett," he repeated thoughtfully. "That's funny. I don't usually refer to my friends quite so formally."

"You have some?" she said with sharp disbelief. "Okay. You want to know? I think some people are probably keeping their fingers crossed that I don't come back."

"What?" The genuine outrage in his tone pierced her defenses.

"You're not the only one who thinks I'm a gold digger, Culver."

"Well, when a woman marries a man that much older—"

"Thank you," she said curtly. "I've heard it all before."

"I don't understand why you would marry him. I mean even if you thought you had to marry for money, couldn't you find a man who was young *and* rich? Good-looking?'' He had lifted himself up on his elbow and was gazing down at her face. ''How could you stand it?'' he asked softly. His finger traced the fullness of her lip.

''Leave me alone.'' But she did nothing to move away from him as his finger stroked her bottom lip with slow and deliberate sensuality.

''I'll bet Elroy never made you feel like this.''

She felt oddly drugged as his lips descended on her like velvet. No, she had never felt anything like this.

Shamelessly her arms twined around his neck, pulling him closer, not understanding what was happening, only understanding it was right. Her very skin tingled with sharp awareness. It was as though the blood coursing through her veins had turned suddenly to fire.

She stared at him, at the broad perfection of his chest. She reached up and touched him with curious fingertips. She had never touched a man in this way before, and it stole her breath from her lungs. He felt good. Strong in all the right places, his skin soft in contrast to the steely muscle rippling beneath it.

His eyes stayed on her face as, unmoving, he let her explore his chest and arms with her hands. His gaze was faintly puzzled.

She wanted only one thing more from this moment. Complete honestly. Complete truth. She wanted him to make love to her, not to Mrs. Pickford.

"I was never married to Elroy," she whispered, wanting him to know he was her first.

He reared back on his arms, staring at her. "You mean you were that old man's mistress?" he finally asked, the ardor gone from his eyes, replaced with contempt.

She gasped. She had trusted him with the truth, and he wanted so badly for her to be something cheap and phony that he had twisted it into what he wanted it to be. Damn him to hell.

She shoved at him with all her might. He rolled off her, but she was not fooled that her strength had moved him.

It had been an act of trust to tell him what no one else in the world knew. That she and Elroy were not married. Hadn't she learned anything over the years?

"I can't believe I ever let you touch me," she snapped with cutting censure. "You know nothing about me."

"Apparently not even your name."

"Oh, drop dead."

He lay awake for a long, long time, the ache he was feeling so deep within him he couldn't just brush it off as lust, much as he wanted to. He had to get them out of here tomorrow. He had to. And not just because they were running low on food.

He looked over at her. She was pretending to be asleep. She was looking more beautiful with each passing hour. How was that possible?

Four

"We have passed that tree twice now," Caroline gasped.

"We have not."

It was another wet day. This morning, he'd started walking, taking big angry strides that she almost had to run to keep up with. His pace had not changed all day.

"I am not going any further with you, Casey Culver. You're mad, and you're moving too fast."

"I am not mad. What would I be mad about?" Unbelievably, he lengthened his stride.

"You're mad because I told you I wasn't married to Elroy." Her voice was coming in ragged gasps.

"Why should I care?" He wasn't even breathing hard! His voice was smooth and indifferent—like he'd rehearsed that line two hundred times inside his own head before he had a chance to say it.

"My thought precisely. Why should you care?"

"I don't."

"Please don't walk so fast."

"I want to get out of here sometime before Santa is coming down my chimney." The gap between them was increasing.

She wasn't asking him to slow down again. She stopped, and folded her arms across her chest. She sat down wearily.

He was so wrapped up in his own little black cloud that it was quite a while before he noticed. He was halfway up a steep embankment, when he glanced over his shoulder.

He was coming back down the incline, his stride filled with muscular grace. And then he was standing above her, looking down, the anger gone totally from his face.

He does care about me, she thought with surprise, taking in every detail of his face with heightened awareness.

"Are you all right?" His strong arms wrapped with comforting tightness around her, his gaze glued to her face.

She nodded uncertainly.

He placed a hard kiss on her lips. It erased her uncertainty.

"Are you ready to go on?"

She nodded again, and found herself being lifted to her feet.

He sighed. "I think we'd better get going," he said gruffly.

Was she falling in love with Casey Culver? she asked herself.

She looked at him. Everything about him had become so familiar to her. The color his hair changed to when it was wet, the thickening beard on his face, the way he squinted when he looked into the distance. He looked strong and proud, rugged and free.

He started to walk again, and her heart followed him, a funny little song singing within its depths.

Her legs could not disobey her heart.

She followed him, something ancient within her telling her what she did not want to know and could not believe. She was his.

They walked for a long time in silence. He did not look back at her.

And then she heard a strange sound. A chill went up and down her spine at the distant wail, high-pitched and eerie. "Culver! Did you hear that?"

A yowl cut the air around them.

He cocked his head. "What the hell is that?"

But Caroline knew. She knew what it was. She turned and ran toward the sound. "I think it's a cat."

"Yeah, right. Domestic kitties all over the place up here. We're a long way from anywhere," he told her, reasonably, racing after her.

It did sound like a cat. They might be close to a house or a cabin. His time with Caroline might be done. He should be dancing, he told himself severely. But there was funny heaviness settling around the region of his tough old heart.

It might be over.

He broke into a clearing. He stopped short, staring with disbelief.

A falling down little cabin stood at the center of the rough clearing. And on the porch of that cabin was a scraggly cat, thin and filthy, its hair tangled like some wild thing. She'd scooped it up and was cradling it in her arms.

She looked like a Madonna.

He did not like the tender feeling the scene caused in his chest.

"Watch it," he said, moving past her to the cabin door. "You'll probably catch something from that filthy thing."

The cat narrowed its eyes and hissed at him.

The cabin was dark inside. And cold. His eyes adjusted to the murkiness. The cabin was very small. It had a main room, a primitive kitchen in one corner of it, a single bed in another. A big black wood-burning stove was dead center of the rough-boarded floor. The furniture was homemade, heavy and rough.

Caroline came in behind him, the cat purring heavily in the circle of her arms. "This poor guy is starving. Is there anything for him to eat?"

"Him?" Culver shot at her. "We might be eating him."

Her arms closed more protectively around the cat. "Casey Culver, you are a caveman."

"And you should be bloody thankful I am, since that has kept you alive, Your Highness."

"Caroline will do quite nicely, thank you."

"What is your last name, anyway?"

"Kenneth," she responded coolly.

"All right, Mistress Kenneth—"

"I knew it would be a mistake to tell you!"

"How about if you put down the royal kitty, and have a look through those cupboards over there?" He went over and opened the stove.

It looked to be in good shape. He saw an axe over the door, and went and grabbed it. He glanced back at Caroline as she squatted and gingerly looked in the cupboards. She pulled back a hand, and looked with horror at a cobweb stuck to her.

"There's powdered milk in here," she said over her shoulder. "If you could bring some water, I could make some milk for the cat."

He sighed and went out the door, slamming it hard behind him. He realized, a little sheepishly, he wanted her to be thinking of looking after *him* not that mangy cat.

He found a woodpile, and set about splitting wood with a vengeance. Despite the fact he was starving, he split wood until his arms ached, and he had to strip off his shirt to keep cool. He hoped the hard physical labor would ease the ache in his loins.

After a while, she sashayed out, and filled her arms with freshly split wood. The cat followed her. He ignored them both.

"There was a note about the cat. They tried to find it before they left, but he'd disappeared."

"Humph." He picked up the next log and set it up carefully. *Crack.*

She turned, her arms full of wood, and went back into the cabin.

Caroline crumpled paper and put it in the stove. Carefully, she put small pieces of wood on top of the paper, and some larger sticks on top of that.

She'd found soup powder—she knew how to cook that. And biscuit mix with instructions inside the tin. She probably could put together a meal of sorts.

She lit a match and held it to the corners of the paper she had put in the stove. Flame licked steadily at the wood, and she turned back to the cupboards, continuing her meager inventory.

Then she sniffed the air. She turned around to see smoke billowing out the stove door, and filling the cabin.

A pile of wood hit the floor, and Casey reached by her and adjusted something halfway up the stove-pipe. The fire blinked back to life, and the smoke began to draw up the chimney.

He shook his head and went back outside.

She glared after him. Well, she'd show him. Following the instructions on various things she'd found, she carefully made soup, potatoes and biscuits... and milk.

It was incredibly difficult to regulate cooking on top of the wood-burning stove. She had never given a thought to her ancestors, but suddenly she appreciated women who had lived in different times.

He came in, his skin slick with water, gorgeous and golden. His hair was wet, and she realized he must have cleaned off at the creek.

The biscuits had burned on the outside and were raw in the middle. The potatoes were not much better. The soup and the milk were fine.

The cat seemed very happy.

He shook his head. She looked embarrassed... and hopeful, like a new bride serving her husband her first effort.

She smiled up at him, a smile that threatened to break away a large chunk of ice that had been building around his heart for a long time. A strand of hair was falling over her forehead and she blew it out of the way. That ice around his heart was beginning to feel like it didn't have a fighting chance.

She sat across the table from him, watching with strange appreciation as he dug into that food with his huge man's appetite. He ate his food, and then sipped with obvious contentment at the hot chocolate she brought him.

His gaze had gone to that narrow little bed. She wondered if, like her, he was wondering what their sleeping arrangements would be tonight.

"Casey," she said suddenly. "What brought you to the north country?"

"Same thing that brings most people. Money brings us," he said slowly, "But there's no telling what makes us stay. Believe it or not, this country grows on you. It starts creeping into your soul. You start to feel homesick when you leave here." He glanced at her. "This is where I'm needed."

"Needed?"

"Yeah. Sometimes the only link some of these settlements have with the outside world is through a bush pilot. You bring the mail and the meat and the medicine. I like being needed in that way. It makes me feel good about myself. It makes me feel like I count."

So he was not like Bill, after all. Not in any way. But hadn't she already known that? Hadn't she suspected for some time that a big heart beat under his bristling surface?

She got up abruptly. The way his eyes rested on her boded very badly for both of them unless she took the situation in hand immediately.

"Which of us gets the bed?" she asked.

"Does it have to be that way?" he asked, the light burning animal bright in his eyes making rockets go off in her chest.

"Yes, it does," she said, "and you can have the bed." Inside, her heart was clamoring dangerously.

He wasn't a gentleman, she told herself later, after they'd cleaned the dishes. He had taken her offer of the bed.

Unself-consciously, he moved over to it, tugged off his shirt and undid the snap on his jeans. He slipped the jeans over the lean hardness of his hips, the hair-roughened length of his legs.

With sudden embarrassment, she realized she was staring at him. She turned away. She heard his mocking laugh and the squeak of the bed as he climbed into it.

She found one more clean blanket. She set it on the hard floor, folded it in two, and crawled between the fold.

It was a long time before she slept and when she did her mother and father haunted her dreams.

She woke up to her teeth chattering painfully, and Casey crouched beside her. "Are you all right?"

She nodded, but tears came.

He pulled her into his arms, with the blanket, tucking it around her. She felt safe, the way she used to feel when she was a little girl, and her father held her to tell her stories.

"You were calling for your folks," he told her softly, brushing her hair back from her face. "What happened to them?"

"They died." She told him about the accident.

"I remember reading about it now," he told her softly. "I'm sorry."

She looked at him with wide and wary eyes.

"Quit trying to be so brave."

"Why. Doesn't it suit me?"

"It suits you all too well," he grumbled. With a sigh, he stood up, with her still in his arms. "Oh, Caroline, come to bed."

He crossed the room with her, and put her down on the bed. He lifted the corner of the cover and slid in beside her. His body felt big and strong and warm.

He turned suddenly and she found her eyes locked with ones that were very blue. "I missed having you beside me, all warm and soft," he said.

He held her tight. She was acutely aware of how her breasts were crushed into his chest, the way his breath was stirring the side of her neck.

"Tell me the truth, Caroline," he whispered, his lips trailing fire down her neck. "Did you miss my body next to yours?"

"Most certainly not," she whispered. "And quit doing that!"

"Most certainly not," he taunted. "Not until you tell me the truth."

His lips took hers, and her resolve melted to nothing as they joined and tangled and danced.

"Okay. I missed it," she said.

He laughed throatily. "I never thought I'd hear the day."

Her lips answered the temptation of his with a heated taunt of their own.

Five

Caroline's lips met Casey's with heated invitation. When she looked up at him, her throat went dry with passion. He was shirtless, his chest hard and broad, his arms corded with sleek muscle. The finest film of perspiration shone on his skin.

She wanted to be possessed by him.

When he bent his head to her breast there was no fury in his lips, only exquisite tenderness as he took her swollen nipple between his teeth and teased it until she writhed against him like a wild thing.

The world was actually tilting crazily underneath her. She almost laughed aloud. Of course, she'd read about such things, but never would she have believed that the whole world would shift, that—

"Hang on!" Casey said, wrapping his arms tight around her as the bed crashed to the floor. It hit with a thundering boom that shook the foundations of the little cabin.

From somewhere under the wreckage of the bed came the yowl of the cat.

Casey closed his eyes, as if asking for strength. She watched him run a frustrated hand through the tangled gold strands of his hair.

His eyes opened. The merest glint of humor shone in them. "Are you all right?"

She nodded uncertainly. If she was all right, why did she have this awful feeling she was either going to start laughing or crying?

The cat continued to make anguished sounds.

"Where is that cat?" she asked.

"Voyeur. He's getting what he deserves."

She clumsily disentangled herself from the bedding, and slid to the floor.

"Culver! He's trapped under the mattress."

Casey heaved the mattress out of the way. She expected the cat to shoot out, but he just lay there mewing pathetically. Caroline reached in and picked him up.

They moved over to the kitchen table, and she handed Culver the cat. He took it with grave reluctance. Turning from him she put some powdered milk in water and put it on the stove to heat.

She turned back to Culver and her mouth fell open with dismay at the look on his face as he looked at the cat.

"What's wrong?"

"I think his front right leg is broken."

"No!"

"I'm not a doctor, but look at this."

Caroline was not a doctor either, but she could tell there was something very wrong with the angle of the cat's leg.

"What are we going to do?" she asked imploringly.

"Caroline," his voice was gruff, "I don't think there's much we can do."

She looked up at him and her eyes were full of hope.

"Okay," he said, "I'll try and splint the leg. I'm not promising any miracles."

"Thank you," she breathed. "You won't be sorry."

The hairball cat picked that moment to swat him with his good paw.

"I already am," he claimed. "See if you can find me something to splint the leg with—a straight stick. And some rags to hold it onto his leg."

She watched how gentle he was as he lay the cat on the table.

He stroked it. "I hate cats," he said in a soothing tone. "I'm a dog man myself. You look like you'd make a good meal for a dog." Then, still talking softly, he took the lower and upper part of the cat's leg in his hands. "Hold him real tight, Caroline."

Swiftly he manipulated the bone back into place. The cat shrieked and jerked under Caroline's grip. He laid open her cheek with one swipe of his paw.

"There. It's in." Swiftly, he had the splint on and tied securely. The cat settled down, and glared at them both balefully.

"Appreciative devil," Culver said, wiping the line of blood off her face. He damped a rag, and washed it off.

Then together they made the cat a nest of rags and put him in it. Caroline shed tears of relief when the animal's eyes finally closed.

"Do you want cocoa?" She hiccuped from her little crying bout.

"I'll make the cocoa," he said gruffly. "You sit. Did I ever tell you about the time I had to fly whale blubber out of the far north?"

"No, you never did." She watched him shrewdly as he turned his back to her. The tears had shaken him, she could tell. And she could tell he was doing his utmost to cheer her up.

Something squeezed at her heart as she listened to his silly story. Culver needed children. Her children. Thankfully, he was too engrossed in his tall tale to be looking at her at the precise moment when that thought hit.

"Okay," Culver said sternly, after the story had reached an improbable but thoroughly satisfying conclusion, where naturally he had saved the day, the plane, a settlement of Inuit, and three whales. "Back to bed."

"My Dad used to tell me stories like that sometimes," she said dreamily. "He always used to finish with a song. I don't suppose you'd sing. Please?"

He hesitated and then he opened his mouth and an amazingly rich baritone sound came out. He sang a lively and carefully edited version of "What Shall We Do with a Drunken Sailor?"

"Sing something quieter," she suggested.

He glared at her as if she'd asked him to sell his soul to the devil.

Then he sighed, and his eyes closed. Softly, his voice rich and sad, he sang.

"If I give you my love, will you love me?
Will you walk with me the days of my life?
If I give you my song will you sing with me?
And dance through the years as my wife?
If I give you my heart, will you hold it,
Cherish it as though it were gold?
If I give you my soul, will you keep it,
Safe and warm as the seasons unfold?

Casey opened his eyes and glanced at her. He looked quickly away.

"That was a beautiful song," she breathed.

"It was the only one Cord wrote that I could remember," he said defensively. "He wrote it for his wife. He really cared for her," he finally said gruffly.

"Casey, I'm sure at one time she really cared for him, too."

"So, what happens?" he demanded. "What the hell goes wrong?"

"Maybe they weren't friends first. I think that's what I want," she said gently, covering his hand with hers. "For you and I to be friends. Just friends."

It seemed so simple. It seemed like it truly could be that easy to take that electricity that was causing all the problems from the air between them and make a decision to be friends.

He pulled his hand out from under hers as though she had held a red hot branding iron to it.

"Yeah, right," he muttered.

"Isn't that possible?"

"Sure," he said insincerely. She thought they could take ten steps backward. She thought by just saying the words you could erase the memories of heated lips and soft breasts. She thought you could put your head in charge and that was that. He'd thought that once, too. A long time ago.

A lifetime ago, before the smell of a haunting perfume had filled the cockpit of his helicopter. He was no longer so naive.

He couldn't stand her eyes on his face anymore— enormous, and faintly pleading. *Let's be friends,* they were saying, as if he could ever look at those eyes and forget how they looked when they sparkled with passion.

He swallowed the remainder of his hot chocolate with effort. He got up and went across the room, wishing suddenly it was bigger, that there was a way to put more distance between him and her. They could be friends, he thought cynically, with a continent or two between them.

She clanged a pot behind him. He walked over to the bed to inspect it. The bed frame had been balanced on four tree stumps of slightly varying heights. He hoisted the four logs into his arms and marched out the door.

It felt good to attack the wood, sawing away furiously, getting rid of all that energy her lips had stirred up in his loins. Finally, satisfied, coated with sweat, he went back into the cabin.

She was back in bed, the mattress settled very solidly on the floor. He dropped the stumps noisily beside her. She turned and looked at him, eyes huge in a face that seemed pale against the dark silk of her hair. She looked so sexy.

"I'll fix the bed now," he said.

"Isn't it fine the way it is?"

"Mice," he said laconically, and was rewarded when she scrambled out of the bed like her toe was on fire. Her legs were long and smooth, and shapely.

He gritted his teeth, hoisting the bed frame back onto the stumps with enough strength to be just a little showy. He gave it a little test with his hand, and it seemed sturdy.

"Go to bed," he said to her.

She actually listened, climbing into bed, and pulling the covers up to her chin. She looked warm and drowsy.

He turned away from her.

"But where are you going to sleep?"

"Not with you—friend."

He had to get away from her. Her eyes were tormenting him. So were her lips, and the thrust of those beautiful breasts against the soft, colorful folds of the blanket.

He went out the door. He wanted to slam it behind him. Just friends. Ha.

He slipped the space blanket out of his pocket, found a shelter beneath a tree, crawled under, and let down his guard.

In seconds he was sleeping.

He was washing in the icy creek the next morning, when she appeared beside him. Caroline felt like the sun was begging her to be in a good mood, to barge right past the No Entry sign pasted all over his handsome face. She had fallen in love with him. She did not know exactly where or when, only that it had happened.

"What are you going to do when you get back?" he asked her. She smiled at him, quick and bright, but he could see a funny sadness in that smile, and couldn't help but wonder in what way he was responsible for it.

"I haven't decided."

"I guess you don't have to do anything, do you?"

"I guess not, but I've thought of teaching."

"You like kids?" he said with surprise.

"I love children."

Somehow he'd pictured her being indifferent to kids.

"Tell me about Elroy." He stared straight up at the clouds. He couldn't bear to look at her face though he sensed the quick darting glance she gave him.

"He was kind to me," she said slowly.

He blinked hard against the stupid rage the tenderness in her voice caused him. The man was dead. How could he be jealous of a dead man?

"That's all you're going to say?" he asked. "He was kind to you?"

He could see the hesitation in her, see that she wanted to tell him something else, but suddenly she got up and turned away.

"Why didn't you get married?"

"Pardon?"

"Why didn't you have kids?" he heard himself snapping at her.

"W-what?"

"You and Elroy? Isn't that why an old man hooks up with a young woman? Because he suddenly starts worrying about his name being carried on? Suddenly realizes he needs a brood mare?" He hadn't liked being her friend, anyway. A little devil in him made him keep going. "So what stopped you? The thought that stretch marks might make your next prey a little harder to land?"

She cast him one look over her shoulder, the pain in her face so intense he felt as if he'd been kicked in the stomach. Which was about what he deserved.

She went up the stairs of the cabin as if the devil himself were breathing down her neck.

Six

He didn't take the closed door as a hint, as Caroline had hoped he would. He came in right behind her, his big arms folded over his chest, watching her shrewdly. As if he knew he had hurt her, and he was glad. Well, she wouldn't give him the satisfaction of knowing the hold he had gained on her heart. She pretended to ignore him.

"I'm leaving today," he said.

"Then so am I."

"Not this time."

"Why not?"

"Everything's changed."

No kidding.

"I couldn't leave you out in the bush with nothing. But now you have shelter and food. I know you'll be safe here until I get back. I can go faster without you."

"That's what you've been doing all your life, isn't it?" she asked with a contemptuous sniff.

"How's that?"

"Moving faster because you don't have anyone with you? Life's pretty carefree all by yourself, isn't it?"

"It's pretty bloody peaceful!"

"And lonely, and empty?"

"Not that I noticed."

"You know, all this time you've sat in judgment of me. You've thought I was shallow and superficial, but it isn't me, it's you."

He looked at her for a long time, his face frozen. Then, "So? What do you care if I'm superficial and shallow? It's not as if I'm planning on marrying you or anything."

"Oh!"

"I suppose that's what you're looking for, somebody to warm your bed now that old Elroy's bit the dust. My muscles probably look pretty good after that."

"You're biggest muscle is between your ears. I hate you."

"Great. Then there won't be any problem with my going by myself."

"That's right. I have to stay here and look after my cat." She felt faintly triumphant—but only faintly. Give a man a few muscles and he thought he could have any woman in the world.

"You might as well have something to eat before you go," she said cheerily. She didn't think anyone would hear the brittleness behind that cheer.

She set a frying pan on the stove, then went and took a knapsack off a hook.

"Look," she said in that same, bright brittle tone, "A knapsack. The real thing. Not a dress with a knot tied in the sleeves." She looked at him. He had sat down at the kitchen table. The sun was coming through the window, spinning gold off his gleaming hair.

She longed to go over and touch that hair, to draw his head against her breast, to beg him not to go with harsh words still so hurtful between them. She knew in her woman's heart that if he stayed, if they had one more night, everything would change.

But time was not on her side, and she knew he had to go. As she cooked some food and packed his things, she felt a secret sorrow. She felt like *his* woman. Except, she reminded herself, Casey Culver was not *her* man.

He pretended he didn't notice her, but he did. Noticed the ache each little thing she did for him caused in him. The scene was decidedly domestic. He wanted to reach out as she bustled by him, stop her, take her onto his knee and hold her, as if he could save her sweetness somewhere deep within himself, and draw on it for strength forever.

But he did not reach for her.

They ate gloopy mashed potatoes in silence. The food seemed to have to slip by a rather large lump that had formed in his throat. He noticed she was picking at hers, too, her eyes drifting to his face, and then beyond it, to the window.

The cat gulped his food down like a wild animal, then limped around on his splinted leg looking for more.

Casey checked the pack. And the rifle he'd found in the cabin. He checked everything twice, not wanting to go, not wanting to be the cause of the sadness in those eyes.

Finally, he knew he could delay no longer. If he did how could he leave her at all? She looked up at him, her eyes huge, and then slowly stood. If she asked him to stay, he knew he could not leave her.

She walked him slowly to the edge of the clearing. *Say you're sorry*, a voice urged inside him. "I guess this is it," he said awkwardly.

She nodded, looking down at her toes.

"Goodbye, Caroline," he said softly. He wanted to kiss her. He didn't know how he could, and walk away, too. He turned from the agonizing invitation of her lips and started walking. He stopped and looked back.

She was still standing watching him, her heart in her eyes.

He could almost believe that she had fallen for him. A belief old Elroy had probably shared.

"Caroline!"

Her body tensed, and she shaded her eyes with her hand.

"If you're rescued first, go. Don't wait for me to come back."

He saw her shoulders sag. She didn't watch him anymore. She turned and walked slowly away.

He walked hard and fast, punishing himself for being such a Grade-A jerk. He realized he was whistling the tune he had so reluctantly sung the other night—the song Cord had written for his wedding.

It took her a long time to go to sleep. She had never in her life felt as alone as she felt in the cabin that night.

Go, he'd told her. Don't wait for me.

And she couldn't wait for him. He'd been alone too long. He was too hardened, too wary, too used to having things his own way all the time. A man like that could never be tamed.

He had never, ever come around, anyway. He had never seen her for who she was. Oh, maybe for a second or two, but mostly passion was all he'd surrendered to. She was worth more than that.

She lay awake wondering if she should have said the words. Three small and simple words, too small and simple to change anything about this rough and complicated world, probably. I love you.

It was going to take him a little while to know what he needed and wanted, if he ever did. Was she just kidding herself that he needed and wanted her?

She finally drifted off to sleep. She was awakened that night by the sound of helicopter blades beating the air. She got up and raced out to the porch, her heart beating in her throat. In her wildest dreams she would have never guessed he would be back this quickly.

But Casey Culver was not one of the men coming across the clearing toward her.

"Are you Caroline Pickford?"

She hadn't thought of herself as Caroline Pickford since she'd told Casey her real name, but it all seemed too complicated to explain. She nodded sickly.

"Is Casey Culver here?"

She shook her head. "He's walking out. He just left this afternoon."

"Maybe we can pick him up, too. Do you need some help? Do you have anything with you?"

"Just a cat," she said glumly. "I'll get changed."

"We had a report of chimney smoke from this area this afternoon. We thought it might be the two of you. We found the stranded helicopter yesterday."

She knew by the relief in his tone that Casey had a lot of friends in this north country.

She excused herself, and ducked back in the cabin. She put on a clean sweatshirt and jeans. Something of his to remember him by.

She had this funny feeling in her heart she was never going to see him again. She had this silly wish that she could send these men away, and wait for Casey to come back.

Out on the porch once again, the cat pulled hard into her chest, she looked around with longing in her eyes. She had come to love Casey here in this wild and untamable land. She had felt like she was coming alive, coming home, coming back to herself.

In an amazingly short amount of time, they were airborne. They swooped back and forth in random patterns searching the area. But there was no sign of Casey. She scanned the rugged land until it swam before her eyes.

"Look, we'll take you into Dease. There are people waiting for you."

She felt the weight of her other existence crushing her.

"Go," he'd said.

She closed her eyes and the tears squeezed out. The pilot shot her a sympathetic look.

They landed at the huddle of buildings that passed for an airport. There seemed to be a great bustle of activity.

"I should warn you the press started assembling here when the helicopter was found."

She stared out at the sea of faces, and sighed. Squaring her shoulders she got out of the helicopter. The pilot came around and put a protective arm around her shoulder, and shoved his way through the crowd.

"Mrs. Pickford?"

She winced at the sound of it. When would it be over? When would she be free of Elroy's well-meaning deception?

"How does it feel to be safe?"

"Can you tell us how you survived all this time?"

"Where is the pilot? Is it true he was killed by a bear?"

She gasped at that, and turned to the questioner, but the other pilot, who felt like her friend, kept her going.

"Jumpin' Blue Jays," he said. "It doesn't take them long to twist a few facts, does it? It was released yesterday that the helicopter, not Culver, had been mauled by a bear."

"Mrs. Pickford, where did the cat come from?"

There were flashbulbs going off in her face. The cat was going crazy, writhing in her arms, and digging his claws painfully into her chest and neck. One of Elroy's aides materialized at her elbow, and between him and the pilot she found herself being escorted through the mob to a waiting jet.

"I can't go anywhere," she protested. "I have to know about Casey."

"You can't stay here. We have a doctor waiting in Edmonton to check you over."

"But I'm not sick!"

"And the will can't be read until you're present!"

"Ah," she said with cynical understanding. A flashbulb went off too close to her face, and the cat hissed and tried to climb over her shoulder.

Go, Casey had said. *Don't wait for me.*

Suddenly she felt exhausted and trapped. The din of the press behind her was almost unbearable. She allowed herself to be led onto the jet, and felt relief when the door shut behind her, shutting the roar out. The cat, whom she secretly thought of as Voyeur, calmed down immediately.

In her heart she knew Casey would be all right. She was sure she shared that same bond with him that his brother had shared. She would just *know* if something had happened to him.

Would it be like this for the rest of her life? Would she be bound to some man who lived thousands of miles away, and didn't even remember her name?

"Mrs. Pickford, we'll be stopping in Edmonton to consult with medical authorities, and then—"

"We'll stop in Edmonton to check on the whereabouts of Mr. Culver, the pilot who saved my life. And don't call me Mrs. Pickford, please."

The man looked startled. She realized she had been very malleable when she left here, a cog in a well-oiled machine.

"Yes, ma'am," he said.

"Now turn off that light and leave me alone."

"Yes, ma'am," he said, this time softly, with understanding that told her the mask she had worn so successfully for so long was gone.

* * *

Casey heard the helicopter roaring over, flying low. But he was in thick brush when he heard it, and there wasn't a thing he could do.

He felt furious and frustrated, and then, to his absolute astonishment, he stumbled out onto the road. If the helicopter just made one more swing it would find him!

But it was gone, the steady "whop" of the blades faded in the distance.

He thought of Caroline, alone in that cabin, and walked on. He'd only been walking an hour down the road, when a truck roared into view. He flagged it down.

"I'm Casey Culver," he told the driver. "I've probably been reported missing."

The man, obviously a fisherman, judging by the array of flies hooked into his hat, smiled a big grin.

"Yup, I heard of ya. Glad ya's okay. What about the woman?"

"She's fine, too. Have you got a radio?"

"No, but I believe Mel Tucker might have one. Prospector. Lives about two, three hours from here. Hop in."

"Have you got a map?" He was handed a very bedraggled map. "There's a cabin here—" he marked it carefully "—Caroline Pickford is there. I want you to go to that radio and have help sent to that cabin."

He started to edge back the way he had come.

"Ain't I better take you back to civilization?"

"No." The way he figured it he could be back to Caroline before the helicopter got there. It could well be morning before the rescue team spotted the cabin.

The truck driver obligingly nodded his head, and took off with a great spin of gravel. Casey took off at a trot, something funny and wonderful leaping in his heart.

It took him longer to get back than he thought it would. The morning sun was growing hot. He felt tired and hungry... and so happy when he saw that dark little cabin that he thought he would burst.

But even before he got there, he could sense the emptiness. He knew long before he opened the cabin door that she was not there, that she was gone. He found the signs that a helicopter had landed. Someone had reported the smoke, he guessed. She'd been rescued.

His heart felt as empty as the cabin. He went over to the bed, and noticed she had made it neatly before she left. Was it his imagination or did some of her scent still linger here? He laid his head down, and let the aroma surround him. And admitted he loved her. He didn't care what she had been to Elroy Pickford.

He fell asleep, the blanket that had wrapped her close to his nose.

He awoke to the very sound that had wakened her, hours before, the steady thrum of an approaching helicopter. It occurred to him that maybe she would be on it, maybe she would have come back for him.

Even though he had told her to go.

Cord was the first one off the helicopter. He raced toward his brother, wrapped his arms around him and lifted him way up in the air.

"Where is she?" Casey asked.

"They brought her out last night. I bet she's in Toronto by now."

He'd told her to go if they rescued her first, but he hadn't meant go all the way back east. He hadn't meant that at all.

He kept his emotions off his face. Pesky things. Until a week ago he'd gotten by quite nicely without emotion. It was probably just like electricity. If you'd never had it, you didn't miss it, but once you had had it, it felt hard to survive without it.

"Let's go to Whitehorse," Cord suddenly suggested, "and do some serious celebrating."

"I'm game," the pilot said. "What about you, Case?"

The one thing on earth that sounded least appealing to him at the moment was to head out on an all-guys weekend to Whitehorse.

No, actually there was one other thing that would be worse. To go home to his empty house and his empty bed. To live the hell of seeing her face in his mind after he'd said those last horrible things about her and Elroy. No wonder she'd gone at first opportunity.

Come to her senses, she had.

Just like he would, given time.

"Whitehorse? Yeah, okay. Why the hell not?"

Seven

The damned woman was everywhere, Casey thought, flinging down the box in disgust. He was helping Cord today, and they were about as far north as they ever went, at a little native settlement with a barely pronounceable name.

And the package one of their customers had handed him was wrapped in newspapers—a newspaper with Caroline's picture on it. For nearly two weeks he hadn't been able to pick up a paper that didn't have her picture all over it. Once the news of her adventure in the far north died down, news of that astonishing will had taken over.

The whole world now knew she wasn't Elroy Pickford's wife. And they knew she'd been left without a dime. Though speculation about the role she had played in Elroy's life ran rampant, nobody was talking, least of all not Caroline Kenneth.

Cord came up behind Casey, glanced over his shoulder, and shook his head with irritating knowing.

"Don't say anything," Casey warned him.

"If I was going to say something—"

"Which you aren't," Casey said with a fair degree of menace.

"Which I'm not," Cord agreed amicably, "but if I was, I'd say go after her."

Casey grunted in a fairly good imitation of a moose about to charge. "Mind your own business."

Cord shifted some cargo around. He didn't shift the package with Caroline's picture on it one inch. "You're my brother. I care about you. A lot. This thing is killing you."

Cord considered himself something of an expert on broken hearts now that he had survived his own. It was very irritating. Of course, Casey thought wearily, what didn't he find irritating these days? He tried to tell himself that just his pride was wounded. He'd come to care about that woman somewhat, and she'd taken off at first opportunity. She hadn't even waited to say good-bye. She hadn't even sent him a note.

Why should he worry if she hadn't been left a dime?

That was the story he tried to tell himself. When he was busy like this, loading a plane, he could forget about her... for whole minutes at a time.

Night was the worst. At night, he would lie in his bed and remember her perfume and the way she laughed. He'd remember those huge, gentle eyes. Lord, what passion had done to those already gorgeous eyes! And then he'd remember the hurt in them. No wonder she had left without even saying good-bye. No wonder she wasn't sending any thank you notes.

"Go after her," his brother said again.

Casey sighed. Go after her. That was another of those thoughts that haunted him long after the hands of the clock had crept by midnight.

Within four days of her escape from the North, the whole world knew Caroline had never been Elroy Pickford's wife. But the whole world was just as much in the dark as he was about what she had been to the old man. If she'd never come to trust Casey with the truth what hope did they have together?

Of course, had he ever encouraged her to trust him? Had he ever just asked her 'If you weren't married to the old goat, what were you to him?' Oh no, he'd just jumped to the worst possible conclusion he could think of.

And he knew exactly why. He was afraid of love. He wasn't afraid of much. He could handle bears and blizzards without even raising his pulse. But he'd watched his brother, every bit as strong and big as he was, torn apart by this funny, unpredictable emotion people called love.

He'd known from the first whiff of Caroline that he was in trouble, and he'd fought it with all he had, and for all he was worth.

And it was only now that he was realizing he'd lost. He'd lost a long time ago, and done his best to kid them both into thinking he hadn't.

He thought she'd cared about him, even though he'd been braced against her caring, like a stubborn mule refusing to budge. Had she cared about him?

"Just go ask her. I sure as hell don't know how she felt about you."

Casey realized he'd said the words out loud. He glared at Cord, as if he'd been eavesdropping on a very private conversation.

"Maybe I will," he snapped.

Cord grinned at him with such relief that Casey understood what a complete jerk he'd been for the past three weeks.

It hadn't been difficult to find out where she lived. The address had been right there on some papers filled out by Cord when she'd chartered the helicopter.

He didn't realize how "northernized" he'd become until he faced Toronto. The traffic and the noise and the pace of people made him feel tense. To add to his irritation, he'd put on a sports jacket and tie, and the tie was strangling him.

He had to drive around the same area six times before he found the building! A man who could find his way out of a thousand square miles of bush. And then he had to pass under the scathing eye of a security man who only reluctantly phoned the penthouse apartment.

"He says he knows Mrs. Pickford, I mean Ms. Kenneth."

"Oh give me that damn thing," Casey said, taking the phone. "Is this Mrs. Beckett? I need to talk to Caroline." His heart was pounding—he felt like a schoolboy going to pick up his date for the prom. "Where is she? The other residence? What other residence?" He frowned at the doorman. "Then I guess I need to talk to you, Mrs. Beckett. Yes, ma'am. Thank you."

He passed the phone back to Flute-Snoot, who listened with indignation to the order he was given and then hung up the phone, and very reluctantly pointed Casey to the elevator.

The elevator apparently only made one stop. There were no buttons to press, except the one to close the door. The elevator shot up with stomach-dropping swiftness, stopped abruptly and the door glided open. It opened right into a huge foyer, part of the apartment.

Despite the fact that much of the apartment was being packed, the opulence of the place was still very much in evidence.

To him everything looked very old, and very cold. Instead of intimidating him it only made him want to rescue Caroline even more. That poor woman couldn't be left to live in a museum. Or maybe now that she'd been disinherited, she had no place to live at all.

A plump, white-haired woman in a flowered dress came out of a back room, apologetically brushing dust off her hands before extending one. She shook his hand warmly.

"I'm Mrs. Beckett," she said. "As you can see, you've caught us at a bad time."

"Us?" he said hopefully.

"I'm sorry," she said. "I didn't mean to imply Caroline was here. She's not." She studied his face for a moment. "You look very tired. Would you have tea?"

"Where is she?"

"She's in the country, helping pack the other house."

"Is it far from here?"

"Come have tea." She led him through the grand rooms and he glared critically at the huge chandeliers, and heavy silk curtains and delicate porcelain statues.

"You've come a long way, haven't you?" Mrs. Beckett asked gently. He nodded.

The kitchen was homier than the other rooms, and she gestured to a stool at the counter. She bustled around, happy, he suspected, to have someone to look after.

"Are you the pilot she was stranded up north with?"

Hope flickered in his heart.

"Did she mention me?" he asked, taking a sudden interest in his thumbnail.

The kindly woman shook her head, and arranged tea things in front of him. "Not by name."

"Oh." So, it hadn't meant anything to her. He'd just been the pilot, a generic term that made him interchangeable with every other pilot on earth.

The kettle whistled shrilly, and Mrs. Beckett unplugged it, her voice very clear in the ensuing silence. "I knew, though."

"Knew what?" He wished he could think of a way to escape here without having the tea, after all.

"I knew something—or someone—had changed her. She was a girl when she left, for all that she looked like a woman. And when she came back she was a woman, for all that she looked like a girl." She smiled. "She walked in here with no makeup on and scratches on her face, in baggy blue jeans and a man's sweatshirt. Her hair was in a ponytail. I wondered why she hadn't stopped somewhere to pick up some decent clothes. I did wonder about that."

"We didn't do anything," he heard himself saying, and then wished he could kick himself.

"Didn't do anything?" she said softly. "Unless I'm very much mistaken, Mr. Culver, you did do something. You fell in love with Caroline."

He stared at the woman, wanting to deny it, but not being able to. He found himself being glad that among all the cold beauty of the things in this apartment, this woman had been here, with her warm eyes and her kind heart, for Caroline. He thought he should probably deny he loved her, but somehow he couldn't.

"Uh," he said uncomfortably, "I was just in town. I thought I'd look her up. That's all." He got up uncomfortably. "Nice meeting you."

"You haven't had your tea yet." She poured it into a very delicate looking tea cup.

Unless he was mistaken there was a certain stern note of iron in that voice. He sank reluctantly back down.

"So I haven't." He eyed the cup warily. If he ever saw Caroline again, he was going to kill her for putting him in this predicament.

"So," he said casually, "what is she going to do? Now that she doesn't have any money?"

Mrs. Beckett laughed. "Don't tell me *you* believe the gutter press?"

He had the decency to look ashamed.

"Caroline has plenty of money. Her parents left it to her in trust when they died."

He was acutely aware that he had wanted her to be desperate so she would need him. And then he realized it would be far better for both of them if she came to him because she wanted him.

"But why all the stories?"

"You should ask Caroline."

A horrible voice in the back of his head was calling him names. Like goon. How he'd made her suffer because of his judgements. Unfounded judgments. Judgments based on a few paragraphs in a rag that was headlining a 72-pound baby born to a 103-pound woman this week.

"Where is she?" he asked. He had to find her.

An approving glint had entered those kindly eyes.

"She's at Elroy's country house. I'll give you a map."

"Thank you, ma'am."

* * *

Caroline walked slowly up the path, through a thick stand of trees, toward the river. She didn't go far, only far enough to feel alone, to leave the bustle of the big house behind her.

It had not been as she had hoped. She had volunteered to help put Elroy's things in order, hoping it would keep her busy, keep her mind on other things. Instead, she was finding it depressing. She did not want to live out her life in this kind of world, empty despite the fact it was brimming full of priceless possessions.

It was not that she was unhappy here. Her days were too full for thoughts of happiness or unhappiness. There was so much to be done. No, it was that there was a funny little ache of loneliness in her that did not go away.

She had come home thinking she could make the ache go away, only to find this was no longer home. The expression was painfully true. Home was where your heart was. And her heart had been given into the keeping of that pirate. He'd taken it as plunder, stolen it with ease, and then just waltzed away and never looked back.

She sighed. She thought of the blue of his eyes, and the black of his whiskers, and the wheat gold of his hair. She thought of his hard chest, and long, muscled legs, and rippling arms. She thought of the way he looked when he laughed, of the way passion smoldered in his eyes.

She thought of what could have been, had he loved her back. Actually, she suspected he had loved her back, but that pride had not allowed him to say so. He had not had the courage to give his heart in trust to another.

He was not the only one with pride. She had bitten back the temptation to send him a little card or a note at least four hundred times.

She pulled her legs up close to her and hugged her knees. Through the tiny hole in the canopy of leaves above her, she could see a star wink to light in the twilight sky.

She made a simple wish. For courage. For love. Silly. Romantic. And yet her wish made her feel better, took some of that sadness from her heart.

Then suddenly rising out of the thick green world around her came another sound. Came and was gone.

She laughed shakily. Now she was hallucinating. She must be more tired than she realized.

She got up and brushed off her skirt, then froze. The sound came again, deep, hauntingly familiar, whispering through thick leaves, calling her.

"If I give you my love, will you love me?"

She was imagining things, of course. She was utterly alone here.

"Will you walk with me the days of my life?"

She turned a slow circle, searching for the source of the song, but the whole forest seemed to be whispering with it.

"If I give you my heart, will you hold it?"

"Casey Culver," she said, her voice shaking, "you come out! You nearly scared me half to death."

And then he slipped out of the trees and was standing far down the path, big as a rock, his arms folded over his chest, the darkness keeping his face in shadows.

She stared at him. It seemed like a mirage, a treacherous illusion, the longings of her mind gone wild. It couldn't be true. Casey Culver would never wear a suit!

If this was insanity, she hoped it would last forever. She ran down the path toward him, stopping short of him, her eyes drinking him in with fierce hunger.

"What are you doing here?"

"I brought you this." He held out something to her.

She took the tiny scrap of paper. "What is it?"

He cleared his throat. "An ad for a teacher. They always need teachers in the north. You said you might like to teach someday."

The paper trembled in her hand. She jammed it into her pocket. "Well, thank you."

"And I wanted to know about that dumb cat."

"Voyeur? He's fine. He likes climbing curtains. You did a great job on his leg."

"And proposing," he said casually.

His face was clean shaven, his hair gold as the sun, his eyes bright and thirsty on her face.

"Proposing?" she whispered. Now she knew it was a dream. Casey Culver, in a suit, talking about teaching and cats and getting married all in the same breath.

He grinned at her and then with endearing shyness held out his arms to her. She flung herself into them. She started to laugh. He was real. There was nothing make-believe about Casey Culver.

"So, will you?"

"Will I what?"

"Marry me!"

"Casey, we barely know each other." It soothed her conscience to say something so rational, when she knew she was about to do the most irrational thing of her whole life.

"I know."

"I have all kinds of money, and you're such a proud man."

"I guess we can work something out."

He laughed, and his arms tightened around her. She gazed into the blueness of his eyes with wonder, that old familiar thrill starting at the center of her and vibrating outward. She stretched upward and kissed him with naked longing.

"If you had all that money, why on earth were you with Elroy? You weren't his mistress."

"No. He was a friend of my parents. After they died, I did some very foolish things, including getting myself engaged to a man who had eyes only for my bank account. So Elroy told two big lies. The Caroline-has-no-money lie got rid of Bill, and the Caroline-is-married-to-Elroy lie got rid of anybody else like Bill. Elroy gave me a chance to grow up."

"You've grown up beautifully," he told her. "Caroline, why did you go?"

"I had to think," she said. "I didn't know if I loved you or if I was just overwhelmed by what we'd been through. And I certainly didn't know if you loved me."

"I did. But I'm so stubborn I'm stupid with it. I couldn't get past the thing with Elroy. Because I didn't want to. I'm sorry. Can you consider marrying a stupid man?"

"Stupidity is often curable," she whispered huskily.

"That means you're going to marry me, doesn't it?"

She laughed at the expression of boyish wonder on his face. "Yes, Casey Culver, it means exactly that!"

He let out a whoop, picked her up, crushing her into the hard wall of his chest. He swooped around with her.

He set her back down. "The first time I smelled your perfume I knew I was in big trouble. All along, I felt this deep need to trust you—to give you my heart, but I fought it because I'd seen what happened to Cord. I'd seen him lose his power to a woman, and I couldn't see myself being in that predicament. I guess I didn't want to believe what my heart was telling me, what it told me from the very beginning. That when people genuinely care about each other, no one loses anything. Everyone gains, everyone wins. My heart tried to tell me that you were trustworthy. Good. Unbelievably good."

"I'm not that good," she teased. "There's a bad girl in me, just dying to get out."

"Let's let her out," he said, leaning toward her.

Her lips eagerly answered the ageless call of his. The call to be joined together in love. The call to walk through life with another. The call to risk her heart.

"Damn," he breathed, "I can't believe we've waited this long. How soon can we get married?" he asked mournfully.

"As soon as you ask me properly."

"It's much more fun to be improper," he told her wickedly, and his big hands went around her waist, and he tossed her over the powerful spread of one of his shoulders.

She laughed and pounded on his back. He ignored her, singing pleasantly:

"If I give you my heart will you hold it?
Cherish it as though it were gold?
If I give you my soul, will you keep it,
Safe and warm as the seasons unfold?"

"Safe and warm, Casey, until we grow old," she promised him. "Now put me down."

"Not until I find a cave."

His. And her heart sang at the refuge it had found.